Keep Your Ear on the Ball

Genevieve Petrillo • Illustrated by Lea Lyon

TILBURY HOUSE PUBLISHERS

Gardiner, Maine

Davey looked like every other new kid that ever came into our class. Ms. Madison walked him in and said, "Boys and girls, this is Davey." He was medium height. He had medium brown hair and medium brown eyes. A regular kid.

Davey looked up at Ms. Madison,
"Mind if I look around?"

"Let me show you to your seat, first," she said.
She walked him to a desk in the first row, right next
to me.

Davey dropped his book bag on his desk and walked back to the door. We all watched as he touched the door frame and the teacher's desk. Then he walked along the bookshelf that went to the back of the room. He ran his hand over the Writer's Center, touched the coatroom doors, the fishbowl, and the library shelf.

He followed
the front blackboard
till he got to his row,
and sat in his seat,
moving his book bag
to the floor under his desk.

He turned to me and said, "It's awfully quiet. Is everybody staring? I'm blind, I'm not an alien!"

That was how we met Davey.

Davey did everything we did.
When we read our books, he read his Braille books.
When we wrote, he wrote on his Braillewriter.
He was a great listener and raised his hand a lot
to answer questions.

"I'm Peter," I said, lining up behind him for lunch. "Want to hold onto my hand on the way to the cafeteria?"

"Thanks, but no thanks," he said.

He followed the line and somehow found a seat at our lunch table.
In the cafeteria, everybody wanted to help Davey.
"Let me open that," Susan said.

"Want me to throw away your garbage?" Amanda asked.
"Should I get you a straw?" Megan offered.
Davey said, "Thanks, but no thanks" at least a hundred times.

After lunch, Davey came outside with our class to the kickball field.
He stood with the rest of the kids as Colin and I chose teams.
He was the first one I picked. "I'll take Davey," I said.

After we finished choosing up sides, Davey went out into the field, and stayed out of everybody's way.

When it was his turn to kick, Davey missed the pitch a million times, and some kids started complaining that he was taking too long.

Amanda said, "Davey, do you want me to tell you when to kick?"

"Thanks, but no thanks," Davey said.

He finally kicked a foul, but he ran toward first base anyway, knocking William down along the way and missing first base by a mile.
Colin took William to the nurse. After that, the game fizzled out.

As we walked into our classroom, I asked, "Do you want me to put your lunchbox away, Davey?"

"Thanks, but no thanks," Davey said.

Little by little, we all stopped asking Davey if he needed help. We were tired of hearing, "Thanks, but no thanks." Most of the time he was fine on his own. Watching him walk around the classroom and through the hallways, it almost seemed like he could see.

He sang with us in music class and made projects with us in art.

But on the playground, it was a different story.

"Can I kick for you, Davey?" Jason asked, after watching Davey miss his first ten kicks.

"Thanks, but no thanks," Davey said.

"I can hold your hand when you run," Amanda suggested.

"Thanks, but no thanks."

After a while, neither captain wanted Davey on his or her team.

"You take him," Daniel whispered as Davey stood on the sidelines.
"I had him yesterday," Amanda whispered back. "You take him!"
Davey settled it. "I'm blind. I'm not deaf," he said. He stormed across the playground and sat on the steps near the door.

"Now look what you did!" Amanda said. "You're mean."

"Why won't he let us help him?" Colin said. "He can't see the ball, he can't see the bases, and he won't let us do anything for him."

"I told him I would kick for him," Jason said.

"I offered to hold his hand and run with him," Amanda said.

"Wait a minute, guys," I said. "That's it! He doesn't want us to do things FOR him. He wants to be able to do things for himself."

"He can't see!" Colin said. "How can he play kickball? How can he do ANYTHING?!"

"He hears and he feels," I said. "He does everything by sound and touch. I have an idea."

The next day, we ate lunch fast, eager to get outside.

Colin picked Davey first on his team. When Davey got up to kick, we were ready. Amanda blew a whistle. Everybody stopped talking and stood still.

Before I pitched, I called, "Here it comes, Davey. Keep your ear on the ball."

I bounced the pitch and in the silence we could clearly hear what Davey heard as the ball headed his way.

We all wanted to yell when he kicked it, but we didn't.
William was standing behind first base. "First base, Davey!"
he called. "First base! First base!"

Davey ran straight toward his voice
and knew from the sound when to stop.

When Davey was safe at first, William moved to second base, and we all yelled and cheered like we'd just won the World Series, till Amanda blew the whistle.

Davey made it to third base before he was tagged out heading home. He joined his team with a smile.

"I'll do better next time!" he said. "Next time I'm going all the way."

"Do you want to wear
the whistle Davey?" Amanda asked.
"You can blow it whenever
you need to keep your ear
on the ball."

"Thanks, but...."
Davey began.
"Thanks, Amanda.
Thanks."

TILBURY HOUSE, PUBLISHERS
103 Brunswick Avenue, Gardiner, Maine 04345
800–582–1899 • www.tilburyhouse.com

First hardcover edition: April 2007
10 9 8 7 6 5 4 3 2 1

First paperback edition: July 2009
10 9 8 7 6 5 4 3 2 1

To Cyndy for reminding me that, "Writers write!" And to David for helping his teacher to learn. —GP

To Carlie, Erik and Ryan. With thanks to Nancy Lum, Teacher for the Visually Impaired, and Ms. Jennifer Brouhard's class at Glenview School in Oakland, CA, for being my actors and models for this book. Special thanks to Laurence (Davey), Kelvin (Peter), and Shannon (Amanda) as well as Mohammed, Leah, and Randall. Francey Liefert of the California School for the Blind connected me with this wonderful group of kids. I couldn't have illustrated this book without them. —LL

Library of Congress Cataloging-in-Publication Data
Petrillo, Genevieve, 1952-
Keep your ear on the ball / Genevieve Petrillo ; illustrated by Lea Lyon. —1st hardcover ed.
     p. cm.
Summary: Davey, a blind student, refuses all help from his new classmates, even while playing kickball
at recess, until they find a way to help without doing everything for him.
ISBN 978-0-88448-296-3 (hardcover : alk. paper)   ISBN 978-0-88448-324-3 (paperback: alk. paper)
[1. Self-reliance—Fiction. 2. Blind—Fiction. 3. People with disabilities—Fiction. 4. Ball games—Fiction.
5. Schools—Fiction.] I. Lyon, Lea, 1945- ill. II. Title.
PZ7.P44685Kee 2007
[Fic]—dc22   2007000108

Designed by Geraldine Millham, Westport, Massachusetts
Printed and bound by Worzalla Publishing, Stevens Point, Wisconsin